Feathers Of Fate

Grimm Academy #9

Laura Greenwood

CONTENTS

BLURB

Helena has known the man she's going to marry for as long as she can remember, and can't wait to leave for the wedding.

There's only one problem. On the way to finally being with him, her prophecy is supposed to come true, trapping her in the life of a goose girl before she can become Wilhelm's wife.

Can she escape her fate?

-

Feathers Of Fate is an academy retelling of The Goose Girl and part of the Grimm Academy series. It includes a sweet m/f romance.

CHAPTER 1

I flip the page of the book in front of me, trying to find the passage I need for my history class. I'm sure it's in this one, but I haven't been able to find it yet.

I pick up my teacup and take a drink, trying to centre myself on my studies.

"Rapunzel, I think I found the book you were looking for," Ella says, handing it over to the dark-haired girl opposite.

Rapunzel gives a relieved sigh and takes it from her. "Thanks. I've been searching for it all week but nothing seems to be where I thought it was."

"Weren't you complaining about the same, Helena?" Ella asks me.

I nod. "I've been searching for a chapter on the Borderlands Trade Deal. I was sure it was in this book, but I haven't found anything yet."

"Maybe the library's been cursed," Rapunzel jokes.

"And all of the books have swapped contents?" Ella adds.

I let out a small laugh, amused by the ridiculousness of my friends' suggestions. "Weirder things have happened at Grimm," I point out.

"That's true," Ella agrees. "I did throw a shoe at my stepmother."

"With good reason," Rapunzel reminds her. "If you hadn't, your prophecy may have come true."

"I know. It's still a little bit ridiculous though," she admits. "But that's the nature of prophecies."

An uneasy smile stretches over my face. It's easy for the two of them to make light of prophecies, they've both managed to avoid theirs already. But mine is still to come, which makes joking about these things a little more difficult.

A servant comes over with a small tray in her hands.

"Princess Helena," she says, dipping into a curtsy. "There's a letter just arrived for you." She holds out the tray.

Sure enough, a small envelope with my name written in familiar handwriting sits on it.

"Thank you." I reach out and take it, my heart racing as I take it. I don't need to open it to know it's from Wilhelm. My betrothed may not attend Grimm Academy, but at least he writes to me regularly.

"Can I get anything else for you?" the servant asks.

"No, thank you," I respond, eager to get to my letter.

"Actually, we wouldn't mind some more tea," Rapunzel says, gesturing to the pot. "And some biscuits, if you don't mind."

"Of course, my lady." The servant dips into a curtsy again and hurries off to do as she asks.

"It's a long time until dinner," Rapunzel says.

Ella lets out a small laugh. "I'm not complaining. The biscuits here are better than the ones our cooks make at home."

I don't pay them any mind and tear open the letter. I know I won't be able to focus on anything until I've read it and started my reply.

I scan the words, eager for news from Wilhelm's kingdom. Most of our courtship has been by the exchange of letters, though I've seen him at least once a year since we met when we were seven. But I feel like I've really got to know him in that time.

Maybe I'm kidding myself, but I don't think so. Our letters have made it possible for us to form a relationship with one another despite the fact we live so far apart.

I scan the letter, anxious for news, only to let out a small squeak when I come to the line I've been waiting to read.

Father says they've finally finished negotiations. You'll be able to come within a month, I can't wait for you to get here.

My hand flies to my mouth, trying to put the sound back in, but it's already caught the attention of my friends, who are both looking at me as if they expect me to combust. I should be glad Briar and Marigold are in class, or I'd have twice the amount of scrutiny on me.

"Is everything all right?" Rapunzel asks.

I manage a nod while I search for the words. "I'm getting married."

Ella chuckles. "We know that. You've been betrothed to Wilhelm for as long as I've known you."

A small gasp comes from Rapunzel. "Unless it's not Wilhelm she's going to marry."

"It's Wilhelm," I assure them both. "He says our fathers have finished negotiations, so we should be able to get married within a month."

"That's great news," Rapunzel says. "Why don't you seem happier?"

I sigh and set the letter on the table in front of me. "I *am* happy. But I'm also scared."

"Your prophecy?" Ella guesses correctly.

I nod. "I want to marry Wilhelm, more than I've ever wanted anything. But I can't shake the dread that comes with the prophecy. It's always been hanging over me, but this is the moment where it's real. My prophecy is about to start, and I'm not sure what to do about it."

Ella reaches out and takes my hand in hers, giving it a soft squeeze. "It's going to be all right. All four of us have been through ours and come out the other side."

I give her a weak smile. "Maybe I'm the one who is going to lose out."

"Not possible," she says quickly. "You have the advantage of knowing how we all managed to stop our prophecies, now you can put that to good use."

"None of you were threatened with spending the rest of your lives as a goose girl," I point out.

"No, but Gavin nearly ended up blind because of his and Rapunzel's prophecy, Marigold ended up enchanted by a scheming frog, and Briar nearly ended up in an eternal sleep. None of that is particularly good anyway."

"Besides, you also have Wilhelm waiting for you when you arrive. He's never going to marry someone else when he could have you," Rapunzel points out.

"That's part of the problem. Our customs say that I need to wear a veil from the moment I arrive in their kingdom, until the moment I'm married," I say.

Ella frowns. "But Wilhelm already knows what you look like."

"And surely your parents won't enforce that given your prophecy," Rapunzel adds.

I shrug. "I've said both of those things to them, but they won't have any of it. According to them, this is the way it's been done for centuries, so this is the way I'm doing it. Mother thinks it'll be bad luck if I don't."

"It'll be bad luck if you do and your prophecy comes true," Rapunzel mutters.

Ella shoots her a dirty look, but I just laugh.

"She's not wrong," I point out.

"I know, but it's still not a nice thing to consider," Ella says.

"Maybe not. But it is what it is. I can't risk damaging the treaty just because I don't want to wear a veil. Not after it's taken so long to put together."

"Why *has* it taken so long?" Rapunzel asks. "You've been visiting one another's kingdoms for your entire life."

"I've no idea, to be honest. I think it might be something to do with an ancestor. Neither of us have ever been able to get our parents to tell us the answer."

"Ominous," Ella says.

"A little. But it's not like there's anything I can do about it. I suppose I could refuse to marry Wilhelm, but I don't actually want to do that."

"Naturally," Rapunzel agrees.

"So that's what it is." I glance at the letter again. I'm sure there's more in it that needs my attention, but I can't focus on any of that right now.

"That means you're leaving us soon," Ella says.

I nod. "As much as I wish I could stay here and go to Wilhelm's kingdom, it isn't an option."

"We're going to miss you," Rapunzel says.

"Same. But I'll still be able to visit, and you'll always be welcome to come to us." It'll be easier for the two of them and Marigold than it will be for Briar. She's going to be a Queen in her own right and busy running a kingdom. But I know we'll all make it work. The bonds we've forged at Grimm Academy are strong enough for that.

"What happens now?" Rapunzel asks. "How long have you got until you leave?"

"I've no idea," I respond. "This isn't an official summons, it's just Wilhelm telling me that they've finished and it'll be soon." I let out a loud sigh.

I wish they all thought to include me more in what's going on. At least Wilhelm feels that he should fill me in on what's gone on so I'm not completely in the dark.

"Then that gives us time to say a proper good-bye," Ella says. "And to make sure we do everything we can to stop your prophecy from coming true."

I smile at my friends, pleased to have them by my side, even if it's just for now.

CHAPTER 2

I drift off to sleep thinking of Wilhelm and how we'll soon be able to spend all our days together. It's been something we've been talking about for years, the fact it can become a reality is both exciting and terrifying at the same time.

As my conscious thoughts slip away, a memory from the past slips into its place. I don't even try and stop it.

No one is paying any attention to me and Wilhelm. The celebrations for the start of a new year are well underway. My parents are busy doing their part as the monarchs hosting the party, and Wilhelm's mother is spending all of her time with a duchess she's friends with.

Which is fine by me. Anything that means I get to spend some actual time with Wilhelm.

"Do you want to go outside?" he asks. "I swiped us this." He lifts up a bottle of wine.

I raise an eyebrow. "You could have just asked one of the servants for it," I point out.

"Where's the fun in that?" A lopsided grin takes over his face.

I shake my head in bemusement. Something tells me I'm not going to have a dull moment in my entire life with him around. Our betrothal is all but sealed, all we have to do is wait for our fathers to finish creating a treaty between our kingdoms. Until then, I'll continue studying at Grimm Academy, and Wilhelm will continue visiting me there, or here in my kingdom for occasions like this one.

Unbidden, my prophecy springs to mind, but I push it to the side. I only learned about it a couple of years ago, and I refuse to let it control my life. Especially not my courtship with Wilhelm. I've not connected with anyone like I have to him, and I'm not going to let any prophecy stand in the way of our happiness.

I grab one of the blankets from a bench. "Come on." I slip my hand into his and pull him through the palace corridors.

No one pays us any mind. They're all occupied with having a good time.

The chill outside air is a welcome change from the oppressive heat of the banquet hall we've come from, and the quiet isn't unwelcome either. Most of the time I get to spend with Wilhelm is heavily chaperoned, unless we're at Grimm Academy, but even then, I get very little actual alone time with him.

Which means I'm going to seize this opportunity and make the most of it.

I lead him under a flower arch and lay the blanket on the ground.

We sit down, close enough that we're almost touching, but not quite. I think we're both a bit nervous about what it may mean to be closer. We've been friends for years, and have known we were going to end up married for almost as long, but something has changed between us in the past year or so, and it's impossible to ignore. When I'm with him, I find myself thinking of romance as well as partnership.

I like it, and I think he feels the same, but I'm not completely sure. Maybe he still sees me as nothing more than a playmate.

Wilhelm pops the stopper off the bottle of wine and hands it to me. "Sorry, I should have thought about glasses."

I smile reassuringly at him. "It doesn't bother me."

Our fingers brush against one another as I take the bottle from him and take a drink.

"That's not very princess-like," he teases.

"Neither is sneaking out into the gardens alone with someone I'm not married to," I point out.

"Ah, true. But what are they really going to do if they catch us?"

I shrug. "No idea."

"Then maybe we should make the hypothetical punishment worth it."

I cock my head to the side and hand him the wine back. "What did you have in mind?"

"A kiss. If you want." The earnestness in his eyes reveals how much he wants it.

I do too. And not because of the wine. I haven't had enough to even slightly cloud my judgement.

Slowly, I nod. "That sounds nice."

Relief rushes over his face, as if he really hadn't been sure whether or not I was going to say yes.

"Are you sure?"

"Yes, I'm sure." I take the wine back from him and dig into the soil of one of the flowerbeds. I'm sure the gardeners will hate me for it, but it'll be worth it.

Wilhelm reaches out, a little hesitant as he tucks a strand of hair behind my ear.

"I'm nervous," I admit, hoping it helps him.

He lets out a small laugh. "Me too. I've never done this before."

"Why do you want to?"

"Because it's all I've been thinking about for my entire visit."

"I think that's a good reason." I shuffle closer to him. "And I've been thinking about it too."

He leans in, and I let my eyes flutter closed, hoping I'm doing the right thing.

His lips press against mine, the touch only a fleeting one, but it's everything I imagined whenever I thought about the fact that one day we'd kiss.

It only makes me more certain that I want to spend forever with him.

We break apart.

A wide smile spreads over my face and my lips begin to tingle. I reach up to touch them.

"Was that all right?" Wilhelm asks.

I nod. "More than all right."

"Same here." He grins widely. "Thank you for letting us try it."

A wave of affection spreads through me and I reach out to touch his hand.

The dream memory slips away before the rest of that evening plays out, but I don't mind. I'll get to spend so much time with Wilhelm that I don't need dreams to feel connected to him.

I shuffle down into my blankets and let myself fall deeper into sleep, with no more thoughts of Wilhelm intruding.

CHAPTER 3

I resist the urge to pace up and down while I wait for the Headmistress to call me inside. This has to do with me leaving the academy and my prophecy starting. It can't be anything else, not after Wilhelm's news.

Nervous excitement fills me and it's impossible to decide which emotion is stronger. As much as I want to arrive at Wilhelm's kingdom and become his wife, I'm also worried about what my prophecy will bring and the dangers I'm about to face.

The door opens and she steps outside. "Why don't you come in, Helena?" She gestures for me to follow her. "Take a seat."

I smooth down my skirt and take a seat, scooting as far back into the chair as I can. I sit as straight as I can, pulling on all of my years of training as a princess to do it. I doubt the headmistress is the kind of woman who can be fooled by a calm smile and a measured pose. For a start, she's taught a lot of us how to do it.

"I'm sure you know why you're here," she says.

I nod. "Prince Wilhelm sent me a letter."

"I'm not surprised. Your parents informed me that the two of you keep contact with one another last time they wrote to me."

"You don't read our letters?"

"Of course not, we believe the privacy of our students is important. Especially when many of them are dealing with their prophecies."

"Oh."

"But you shouldn't worry yourself over that. We need to discuss the arrangements for you leaving the academy tomorrow."

"Tomorrow?" My voice squeaks ever so slightly. "I didn't realise it would be so soon."

"Your future father-in-law is keen to get the marriage contract signed and everything arranged, your parents are too," the headmistress says.

"I see."

"Is anything the matter, Helena?" she asks.

I resist the urge to sigh. "I thought I'd be more excited," I admit. "But now I'm faced with leaving, I'm realising everything I'm losing by going."

The headmistress smiles kindly at me. "You're not losing anything. Your friends will still be your friends even if you live in different kingdoms, and you're still going to be welcome on the academy grounds, you aren't banished once you leave."

"Thank you."

"It's academy policy," she reminds me. "But you're welcome."

I don't respond, unsure what else there is to say. It's conflicting to want to see Wilhelm again, but also want to spend more time with my friends, but I'm not sure what I can do about it. This has been the plan for many years, and I should be excited to think it's going to become reality.

"Is there anything you need before you head on your journey?" she asks.

"Have my parents sent a veil?" I ask.

"Not that I'm aware of. What is it supposed to look like?"

"It should cover my face completely and come down to my shoulders," I say. "I'm not supposed to show my face when I get to Wilhelm's kingdom until we're married."

The headmistress frowns. "I thought you'd already met?"

"We have. But it's a tradition Mother has always wanted me to obey." It seems pointless to me when Wilhelm and his family all know what I look like anyway, but there's no point in fighting it when it's what Mother wants. I suppose I could turn up without a veil to Wilhelm's kingdom, but I'd rather not deal with the angry letters from home if I do.

A knock pulls our attention to the door and it cracks open to reveal a servant.

"I'm sorry to interrupt, Madam Headmistress, but I have a package for Princess Helena and instructions to deliver it right away."

The Headmistress nods. "Very well, bring it in." She doesn't seem very surprised that the servant has come, maybe she already thought something like this would happen.

The servant steps inside with a small package and places it in front of me on the desk. "Your Highness." She dips into a curtsy before turning to the headmistress and doing the same.

I stare at the neat handwriting on the front of the parcel, recognising it straight away.

"It's from Mother."

"Perhaps it's the veil you need. If it isn't, let me know and I'll make sure to have one of the seamstresses pull out some fabric choices," the headmistress says.

"I can open it here and save the time?" I suggest, already assuming that she's right and it is the veil inside.

"If you wish." She leans back in her chair and watches, though it doesn't make me uncomfortable. Whoever decided to put her in charge of the academy made a good choice. She's firm, but still friendly and fair.

I pull the paper away and find a sealed letter. The envelope is heavier than I expect it to be. Despite knowing I should just check for the veil and read this when I'm alone in my room, I tear it open.

A small feather charm on a woven bracelet falls out and I don't need to read what Mother says to know what it is. My friend Briar has a protection charm she wears all the time, only hers is a rose and not a feather. I slip it over my wrist. If Mother wants me to have it, then there's going to be a reason and I don't want to wait to have its protection.

I unfold the letter, my beating heart the only sound other than the wrinkling of paper.

My Darling Helena,

I am sorry that we can't be together on this important day of yours. I thought it could be different but it is not meant to be. I have sent a charm for you to wear on your journey to protect you from the evils that may otherwise befall you. Please keep it on you, we don't know when your prophecy will strike.

I have also enclosed the veil I wore when I arrived at the palace to wed your father. I hope it brings you as much luck in your union as it did to me for mine.

I am sending all the love I have to you. Give blessings to Prince Wilhelm and his family on my behalf.

Your loving mother.

A small tear rolls down my cheek and splashes to the page. The headmistress is blissfully silent as I set the letter down and pull out the heavy lace veil Mother sent me. I've never seen it before, and the fact she's sent it to me now says more than her letter ever could.

"I see we won't be needing a veil," the head-mistress says.

I smile and shake my head. "No, I have my mother's."

I may have reservations about the validity of the practice of veiling brides so heavily, but I'm honoured that I get to wear this, and touched beyond words that Mother is trusting me with such a precious heirloom of hers.

"Thank you for the offer," I say. "I appreciate it."

"You're welcome," the headmistress says. "You should spend the rest of the day saying your goodbyes. I'll arrange for the logistics of travel."

"Thank you." I get to my feet and make my way out the door. There's lots to do before I leave, and that starts with finding my friends.

CHAPTER 4

The fire crackles, filling Rapunzel's room with warmth. Though that may also be down to the sheer amount of food we've eaten. The remains of our small feast scatter the low table, with barely anything left.

"I'm glad you have the big room," Ella says to our friend. "It means we get to say goodbye to Helena without the prying eyes in the dining hall."

Marigold sniffs and I reach out to put an arm around her.

"It's all right," I promise. "You'll be able to visit."

"I know, I just can't believe you're leaving." I can hear the tears in her voice even if she isn't shedding them yet.

I blink away my own. I love these girls. They're my best friends and we've been through so much together, it's sad to think that I won't wake up next week and go down to breakfast to meet them.

But I know this is for the best. I've been betrothed to Wilhelm for so long that it's time for me to get there and become his wife.

"This is pretty," Briar says, reaching out to touch my feather charm. "Is it new?"

I nod. "Mother sent it along with my wedding veil. It's supposed to protect me from harm. Though I'm not sure what good it's going to do."

Briar flashes me an understanding smile. "Mine helped against my prophecy," she reminds me, pressing her fingers against the rose charm around her wrist as she does. I don't think she has to continue wearing it now her prophecy is done, but I like that she does.

"I hope mine will do the same."

"Are you worried?" Ella asks. "About your prophecy?"

I sigh. "More worried than I have been. It's always seemed so far away, and now it's tomorrow. What if I get things wrong and end up spending the rest of my life as a goose girl?"

"It won't go wrong," Marigold assures me.

"It's not even the goose girl bit that I'm worried about the most," I admit, realising I've never said this part out loud. And with good reason. "I'm worried that Wilhelm will like the woman who takes my place better than me."

"Have you not seen the way Wilhelm looks at you?" Briar asks softly. "There's no way he's going to want anyone else."

"Mmhmm. It's never going to get as far as the wedding even if something does go wrong," Rapunzel adds. "He'll take one look at the imposter and know it's not you. He won't marry her then."

"She'll probably be wearing the veil, though. He won't see her face." Yet another reason why I think Mother's insistence on me wearing it for my wedding is foolish. It could be the difference between me stopping my prophecy, and having to live through it.

Not that I ever got anywhere with that argument.

"Wilhelm doesn't need to see your face to know it's you," Marigold says.

"She's right," Briar agrees. "I'd know Walter even if his face was covered."

"But you've spent more time with him than I have with Wilhelm," I point out. "All of you have with your suitors." It's one of the things I've always been a little jealous of. None of them have had to do their courtships via letters, or wait for a meeting once every few months. I'm sure several of my friends will leave this room and go meet their other halves. I don't resent them the love they've found, I just wish I got to enjoy more of my own at the same time.

Marigold reaches out and puts her hand over mine. "It's going to be all right, Helena. Wilhelm isn't going to marry someone else, and you're not going to get stuck as a goose girl. You'll arrive in his kingdom, get married, and have dozens of children running around you in no time."

My eyes widen. "I think that's too many children. And too soon."

Briar raises an eyebrow. "You're marrying a prince, they're going to expect children before too long."

A furious blush rises to my cheeks. "I guess we'll see," I mumble.

"At least there's plenty of fun to be had before then," Marigold quips, gaining amused chuckles from my friends.

"I have to get there first," I point out. "According to my prophecy, the journey is the most dangerous part for me."

"What exactly is supposed to happen on it?" Ella asks. "You've never told us your whole prophecy, just the parts where it relates to you going to marry Wilhelm."

I take a steadying breath. This may be a hard thing to talk about, but it's better than letting them carry on the plans for mine and Wilhelm's non-existent children.

"Basically, on the journey, someone will try to switch places with me. She'll trick me somehow, and go to the kingdom with me as her servant. Once there, she'll marry the prince, and I'll be forced to be a goose girl and sleep in the stables, unable to speak a word of it to anyone unless they already know who I am."

"There's lots of hope there," Ella says. "Wilhelm will recognise you even if you're a servant."

"I'm not so sure. And what if he's kept away from me? There are lots of ways he may not realise that I'm the goose girl." Even thinking about it like this is enough to tie my stomach up in knots. It's not that I don't trust Wilhelm, because I do. It's just that we haven't had enough time to properly get to know one another, and that's something I worry about.

But to some extent, I just have to live with it. I can't change my prophecy, the best I can do is to try and avoid it when it starts coming to pass.

So, tomorrow.

"You need to have faith in yourself," Ella says. "You're stronger than you think, and you'll be able to avoid your prophecy just like the rest of us have."

"But I'm not going to have the four of you around to help me." A hint of sadness enters my voice.

"We'll be with you in spirit," Briar promises.

"And you're the strongest of us all," Marigold adds. "We'll be looking forward to a letter saying everything went perfectly."

Ella nods along, clearly agreeing with what the others are saying.

"I wish I shared your belief in me," I admit. "But thank you all the same."

"That's what we're here for," Rapunzel says. "Though we're also supposed to be having a good time to say farewell, not dwelling on the bad things."

I chuckle. "Sorry, that's my fault. I feel like I'm all doom and gloom."

"We don't blame you," Briar assures me. "And we're going to miss you."

"I'll miss you too," I admit, looking around the room at the assembled young women. "But I'm so glad that I got to meet you. My time at Grimm has been amazing because of you."

"It's the same for us," Marigold assures me. "I'm so glad that I've been able to know you."

A warm glow fills me. There's so much affection in this room, and I feel stronger for being around it. While I'm going to be on my own tomorrow, I know that I have the well wishes of my friends behind me.

I'm sure that will make all the difference when the darkest part of my prophecy comes.

CHAPTER 5

Having listened to an hour-long sermon on etiquette I've known since I was old enough to dance, I'm almost ready to set off and face my prophecy. I don't know why they insist on etiquette lessons being so boring, but I can barely keep my eyes open for them.

Even so, nerves flutter in my stomach, making it clear that I may not be as ready as I want to be for it.

I just have to remember that once I'm through the next day, I'll have everything I've ever wanted and more.

The bell rings, signalling the end of the lesson. I almost sigh with relief. it's not that I want to rush to meet my prophecy, but I hate waiting and now this part is over.

I glance behind me as I leave the room and smile at the dark-haired girl behind me. I think her name is Alyeesah, but I'm not too sure about that, I've never had much to do with her.

I search the crowd of students for my friends, but I know none of them are here. They've all had different classes to me and are in other parts of the academy. It's sad, but at least I got to spend the evening with them yesterday.

I head up to my room to grab my travel bag and stand in the doorway for a moment, unsure how I feel about leaving this all behind. As of tonight, this is no longer going to be mine. I'll no longer be a student of Grimm Academy. It's an odd feeling and one I'm not sure I particularly like.

With a deep sigh, I shut the door behind me and head down to the stables. Knowing the head-mistress' timekeeping, the carriage will already be waiting for me, and I don't want to delay the journey any more than I have to.

Sure enough, the ornate carriage sits with guards mounted behind it. I've been treated like royalty my entire life, but there's something about this that feels extra official.

Another student is riding around the yard, completely oblivious to the fact I'm about to go on a life-changing journey.

I ignore them and head over to the groom.

"Is everything loaded into the carriage?" I ask.

He nods. "Yes, Your Highness. I believe some of your trunks are following behind, though."

I smile reassuringly at him. "They are. It's just me and the most important items going with this trip."

"Not your maid?"

I frown. "I don't have a maid."

"I'm sorry, Your Highness, but there's a young woman who says she's your maid. She's waiting inside the carriage."

A thread of fear winds through me and I wonder what's going on.

"Very well. Please wait for my signal to leave."

"Of course, Your Highness." He dips his head in acknowledgement.

With nerves battering at every part of me, I climb up the steps and through the open carriage door.

"Melanie?" I ask, surprise in my voice.

"Your Highness," my maid responds to the greeting.

"What are you doing here? I had no idea you were coming." I haven't seen her since I was last in my own kingdom.

"I was sent to accompany you as a friendly face," Melanie responds.

"Mother didn't say anything in her letter about it."

"She wanted it to be a surprise. She thought you could use the company for the journey and the support once you arrive in Prince Wilhelm's kingdom."

"Ah, how nice of her." But perhaps it would have been better if she'd thought to tell me in advance, especially with the details of my prophecy to take into account.

But this is Melanie. I've known her for most of my life and I know she isn't going to do anything to hurt me.

"I thought so too," Melanie says.

"And you don't mind being so far from home yourself? Your father doesn't mind?" As the palace blacksmith, I'm sure Melanie's father has more than enough work to keep him occupied, but that doesn't make up for the fact that I'm taking his only child away from him. I hope he doesn't feel like we've pressured him into losing her.

"I see this as one big adventure," the maid assures me.

"Then I'm glad to be taking you with me. But if you change your mind, let me know so I can send you back with a good recommendation."

"Thank you, Your Highness, but I don't think that's going to be necessary."

A knock sounds on the carriage door and the groom pops his head inside. "Is everything all right, Your Highness? Do you need to delay our leaving?"

"No, we're all good to go," I respond. "It's time to get on our way."

"Very good. Would you mind bolting the door from the inside?"

"Of course."

He shuts the door firmly behind him and I reach out to bolt it. I much prefer carriages that have the option to lock them from the inside, it makes me feel a lot more secure about the journey I have to undertake.

Dim shouts come from outside the carriage walls and it starts to move. Between the crunch of the horses' hooves on the gravel drive of Grimm Academy, and the creaking of the carriage, it's almost deafening.

I pull back the curtain and watch the castle as we move further away from it, a sad longing in my heart. The academy has been my main home for the last few years, and now I'm leaving it behind.

I wonder if it'll feel the same for my friends when they leave, or if they'll be too busy celebrating with one another.

Maybe I'll be able to join them for the event. I suppose that's a bridge we will cross as and when the time comes.

"Will you miss it?" Melanie asks.

"More than I ever thought I would." I let the curtain fall back into place and lean back in my seat. "But I'm also glad that I'm going to see Wilhelm."

"You've been sweet on him for a long time."

"It's been eleven years," I say wistfully. "Though I don't think I always thought of him as my future husband." Or I did, but not the kind I could grow to love. For a long time, he was just the fun friend who visited. It wasn't until a few years ago that we started to see one another differently.

But I think that's what makes us so good together.

"You must be glad that you finally get to go marry him," Melanie says.

"I am." I sigh wistfully. "He's a good man, and I'm glad we finally get to spend some proper time together. But I'm still sad to leave my friends behind. I wish I could somehow have it all."

"To some of us, you already do," Melanie murmurs, though the words are so soft that I suspect I wasn't supposed to hear them.

"I know, I have great friends and a wonderful betrothed. I'm luckier than I could ever imagine." I sigh and lapse into silence. I need to be careful not to sound ungrateful for the gifts I've been given. I could be in a lot worse situation than I currently am.

"Precisely."

"Are you not leaving anyone behind?" I ask Melanie.

"No, I'm hoping that it'll be my turn to find a sweetheart once we arrive in Prince Wilhelm's kingdom."

"I'm sure you will, I'm yet to meet anyone who wasn't delightful company from there." She'll probably end up engaged to one of the castle servants before the end of the month, I know things often move quickly with the staff.

"I'm absolutely certain I will." The way she smiles along with her statement makes me a little ill-at-ease, but I can't pinpoint why.

I push it out of my mind and focus on what's important. And what I'm going to say when I finally get to see Wilhelm and know that I don't have to turn around and go home at the end of the visit.

CHAPTER 6

Every now and again I peek through the curtains to see where we've gotten to. Not that I know the geography of the land between Grimm Academy and Wilhelm's kingdom particularly well, but I always find it interesting to see what the world around us looks like.

"I think we're approaching the Fast River," I say to Melanie. "Have you seen it before? It's beautiful."

She shakes her head. "I've never travelled outside our kingdom before," she responds.

"Oh, I'm sorry, I didn't realise. You should look out and see, it's truly something." Green trees line both river banks, with a carpet of flowers reaching all the way down to the glistening water.

"Maybe we should stop and eat some of our picnic?" I suggest.

Melanie shakes her head. "We shouldn't, Your Highness, we're already on a tight schedule if we want to get to the inn before nightfall."

I sigh. "It's a shame, this would have been a beautiful spot for a rest, but I know you're right. Perhaps I should have requested the trip to have taken three days instead of two." Even as I say it, I realise I never would have done. More days means more chances for my prophecy to become true. Once I'm in Wilhelm's kingdom, I should be safe from the people who want to harm me.

"That would have been nice," Melanie says, a hint of something strange in her voice.

I push my thoughts aside and let the curtain fall back into place. It's a shame they don't come with ties so I can leave them open, but it does add a certain element of mystery to the journey when I can't see the outside.

I lean back in my seat and let my thoughts drift towards my arrival at the castle and the people waiting for me there. I can't wait to see Wilhelm's face again, or to feel his kisses, though I may have to wait on that. While we've been left to our own devices for most of our visits to one another's kingdoms, I don't think it's going to be the same when I'm there for the wedding.

Hopefully, his father doesn't prolong things too long when I arrive and the wedding will take place quickly. I don't see why it won't when he's waited so long to send for me in the first place.

A slight bump comes as the carriage rolls onto the bridge, followed by a heavy shake of the whole thing.

"What's that?" I ask, pulling the curtain back sharply and looking outside. As far as I can tell, nothing has changed outside. There certainly aren't any hints of what may have made the carriage rumble like that. "Did you feel it?" I ask Melanie.

"Feel what, Your Highness?" She seems genuinely confused, which makes me start to think it's all in my head.

"I thought the carriage shook. It must not have been anything." Even as I say it I realise I don't believe that's true.

"I didn't feel anything, I'm sorry."

"There's no need to apologise, I must have just been imagining it."

We lapse into silence as we continue across the bridge, and this time it isn't particularly comfortable.

"Do you mind passing me a drink from the picnic basket?" I ask Melanie after another few miles.

"You should get it yourself," she murmurs barely loud enough for me to hear.

I frown, a little confused about why she'd refuse to do something as simple as hand me a drink, especially when the basket is closer to her than me, and she's supposed to be on this journey as my maid. But I shrug it off. She says she's never been this far from home before, so perhaps she's just feeling a bit travel sick. I did the first time I went on a long carriage ride, and the road hasn't been a particularly forgiving one.

I hop over to the other side of the carriage and pull out the picnic basket. A couple of bottles of water sit close to the top. I pull them out and offer one to Melanie.

She takes it without a word and turns her attention to the window on her side of the carriage, confirming what I already suspect. She's travel sick and I should be understanding of that.

The light outside the carriage starts to fade, making me worry about whether or not we'll get to the inn before it's too late.

Just as I'm about to knock to get the driver's attention, the carriage starts to roll to a stop. I break a sigh of relief

I unbolt the door and wait for the groom to make his way around to help me down. Sometimes, I like to hop down by myself, but I don't think it's appropriate given where I'm going.

"Your Highness," he says, holding out his hand. I take it and he helps me to the ground in a graceful motion. "If it's acceptable to you, the guards would like to forgo your title while we're at this establishment," he says softly.

"Of course. They know what's best for safety." I offer him a friendly smile so he knows I'm not offended by the question.

"Thank you, Your...ma'am. I'll let them know."

"Would you help my maid down first?" I ask. "I think she's travel sick and I don't want her to fall when she gets down from the carriage."

"Of course."

He allows me to step aside so he can help Melanie down. I take the chance to check if my veil is still safely inside my bag. I could have packed it in one of the trunks, but I don't want to risk losing something so precious to Mother. Satisfied it's safe, I take a deep breath, enjoying the fresh air. If it was earlier in the day, I'd consider going for a walk to stretch out my sore arms and legs. Carriage travel isn't always particularly comfortable.

After what feels like a small age, Melanie joins me outside the carriage.

"It helps to walk it off a bit," I tell her. "The feeling will go away." Though she probably knows that if she travelled by carriage from my kingdom to Grimm Academy in the first place.

She nods.

I watch as she makes her way around the small clearing in front of the inn. I'm impatient for our journey to end so I can see Wilhelm again, but I know that this break is necessary for us.

But tomorrow can't come soon enough.

CHAPTER 7

I stretch awake, stiff from the uncomfortable bed the inn provided, but grateful I got to sleep in one at all and didn't have to stay awake travelling all night.

I reach out to the bedside table for the feather charm, but my hand comes away empty.

I sit up suddenly, searching for it.

"Looking for this?" Melanie asks.

I turn to face her, finding her sitting at the end of my bed wearing one of my dresses and holding out my charm.

My eyes widen and a sense of dread settles in my stomach. "What's happening?"

"What do you *think* is happening?" A wicked smile twists at the corner of her lips.

"Melanie..."

"I'd rather if you got used to calling me Your Highness. You're going to need to from now on if you don't want to get caught."

"Caught doing what?" My sleep-ridden thoughts try to piece together what she means, but it's not getting very far very fast.

"We're going to be setting off soon, and when we do, I'll be taking the place of the princess, and you'll be my servant."

Oh no.

"Please don't do this, Melanie."

"Your Highness," she corrects. "I see you're going to have to need some training."

"Why are you doing this?" I ask.

"I suppose because I can." She gets to her feet and picks up the dress she wore yesterday and throws it towards me. "You should put this on."

"Why would mother send you if you were going to do this?" Hurt laces through my voice. I should hide my emotions better, but I'm in disbelief over what's happening and that's making it more diffi-cult to do.

Melanie bursts out laughing. "Your mother didn't send me. She wasn't going to send anyone to avoid the risk of triggering your prophecy. It was foolish because it gave me the perfect way to escape life as a servant."

"That's all this is about? Why didn't you engage in a trade?"

"You think it's as easy as that? Once you've been a servant, that's all anyone thinks of you as." The venom in her voice was impossible to ignore.

A small part of me wants to ask her what it will take for her to leave me alone, but the reasonable part knows that there isn't going to be anything. She seems to be projecting her anger over something onto me, and I'm not sure why.

"I want to escape my life, and to do that, I'm going to marry your prince."

"But that doesn't change anything for anyone else."

"What do I care about them?" Melanie shrugs. "I just want a better life for me."

"You're not going to get away with it," I point out. "I know it seems like you're going to, but what about Wilhelm? He's not going to marry you when he realises you're not me."

"You remember we come from the same kingdom, right? I know about the veils. My bet is that your Wilhelm won't even realise he's standing across from someone who isn't you. How many times have you seen each other? A dozen? It can't be many more than that."

Each of her words sends a lance of pain through my heart. She isn't wrong, we've not spent much time together, and while I'm certain Wilhelm *knows* me, whether he'd recognise my voice without my face is another matter.

No. I can't think like that. I have to trust that he knows me better than this.

"You aren't going to get away with this." I throw back the covers of my bed and head to the door, determined to find one of the Grimm Academy guards and tell them exactly what's happened.

Melanie reaches out and catches my wrist in her hand. Her fingers dig into my skin, leaving small marks that I'm certain will take time to fade.

The action pulls me back so I'm facing her once more.

"That's not going to work, Helena," she sneers. "You don't think I'm that stupid, do you?"

"I never said you were." I gulp down my nerves, but I'm sure they still show on my face. "I'm not going to get you into trouble, I just want to get to Wilhelm's kingdom so I can marry him." Even as I say it, I realise she's never going to let that happen. For whatever reason, she's decided that Wilhelm is the answer to her problems. It's selfish and a little foolish, but I think in part I can understand it.

If I leave this room having switched places with Melanie, then all of my hopes are going to be pinned on Wilhelm and whether or not he'll be able to work out what's happened before it's too late.

"Remember that cup of warm milk I brought you before bed?" she asks.

"What did you do to it?" Horror sets in.

"I used a potion that means you won't be able to talk to anyone about who you are, or what might have happened."

A sinking feeling settles within me. This is exactly like my prophecy said it would be. I'm not sure why I thought it would turn out to be different, but a naive part of me thought it couldn't possibly be true.

"You'll only be able to tell someone who correctly guesses your name in the first place. Isn't it perfect?" Glee sparkles in Melanie's eyes. "And no one is going to look at the poor servant and believe that they could possibly be Princess Helena."

I hate to agree with her, but I think she's right about that. There's a reason not many people are ever able to convincingly portray royals, and this is one of them.

"Now, you're going to put on your dress, tie up your hair in a plait, and put some of the soot from the fire on your face. We can't have you looking too clean. I assume you know how to do all of that?"

I nod. Living at Grimm Academy gave me a lot of skills, and being able to prepare myself for the day is definitely one of them. I could have called for a maid to help me at any point, but I always ended up feeling like I was pulling them away from more important tasks for something I really could do myself.

For a moment, I consider not doing what she says and refusing to budge from the room, but I know that's not going to get me anywhere. And it's certainly not going to stop my prophecy before it comes to pass.

My best bet for that is to make my way to Wilhelm's kingdom and hope he works it out. He's known the details of my prophecy since the moment I learned of them. It was before I'd met my friends at Grimm Academy, and he was the closest thing to a confidante that I had. I gladly told him every word.

Hope blooms within me. Wilhelm knows. That means he's going to be on the lookout the moment we enter the gates.

Melanie isn't going to get away with it, even if she thinks she's going to. All I have to do is survive getting there.

My former servant places Mother's veil over her head, causing anger to rouse inside me. If Mother was here, she'd be tearing it off and screaming at the other girl despite how un-Queenly that would be.

But I don't think I'm in a position to be able to do that. I need to focus on surviving, and that means playing by Melanie's rules until I get there.

Her dress itches against my skin where it's too tight, and sags badly where it's too big. I'm sure both of those add to the impression of a poor servant girl she intends to portray me as.

I wrinkle my nose as I smooth the soot against my exposed skin, rubbing some into my hair for good measure. I have to make her believe I'm beaten or there's no chance that I'll be able to stop the worst from happening.

Even so, it's difficult to follow her downstairs and into the carriage that's meant to be for me. None of the guards notice that we've switched places, though that's probably because of the veil more than anything else.

I have to believe that it's still going to be all right. I'll find a way to switch us back without hurting anyone and losing the life I've been waiting so long to live.

I just have no idea how.

CHAPTER 8

Trumpets sound and drums rumble as we roll through the main gates and into the castle grounds. I resist the urge to pull back the curtain to try and get a peek at Wilhelm, knowing that it may end up giving away more than I want to about what's going on and the situation at hand.

Melanie sits up straight and even if I can't see her face, I can sense the smug smile and the thoughts racing through her head.

She's pleased with herself and thinks that this is over. And maybe she's right. The only thing she needs to do once she gets inside is to find a way to send me to the kitchens, the stables, or anywhere else that means I'll never have to be seen.

I try my best not to let my unease show on my face. I don't want her knowing that she's managed to get to me, especially with how smug it's going to make her.

"Remember, you can't talk about who you are," she says as if I could possibly have forgotten. "The woman I bought the potion from wasn't very specific about what it would do if you did, but I can't imagine it'll be very pleasant."

I force a smile onto my face. "Your wish is my command, Your Highness."

"Better, but it still needs work," she mutters. "But it won't matter. You'll learn your new place soon enough."

I don't respond, mostly because I can't think of what to say, but partly because I suspect my silence will irritate her more than it will me.

The carriage comes to a stop and she leans forward to unbolt the door.

"Remember, a few steps behind me with your head bowed and don't say a word."

"Of course, Your Highness." I make my voice as light as I possibly can, but I think it sounds too fake.

Melanie doesn't seem to mind.

The door swings open and a groom helps her down. The veil shifts a little, but she's still wearing it correctly. No doubt she made sure to check up on that sort of thing before she came to take my place as Wilhelm's bride.

Anger bubbles up inside me at the thought of her marrying Wilhelm, but I just have to remember that it isn't actually going to happen. I'm going to find a way to make sure that it doesn't.

I step out of the carriage and fall into step, all the time worrying about what's going to happen next. I have no idea what the consequences of Melanie's plot could be. While she may end up married to Wilhelm in my place, that's only the start of things. My parents could blame Wilhelm's family for my disappearance, and I doubt they'll take kindly to their broken treaty.

Nor will Wilhelm's family if they think mine is to blame for the wrong woman being sent in my place. At worst, Melanie's plan could devolve into a war between our two kingdoms. I doubt she's thought about that, especially as she seems to be on a personal vendetta that has nothing to do with understanding the intricacies of inter-king-dom politics.

One thing I don't think she understands is that it isn't her low birth that makes her an unworthy princess, but her selfishness.

We approach the steps of the castle where Wilhelm and his parents wait. My heart skips a beat as I recognise the familiar figure of the man I hope to marry. He looks exactly the same as the last time I saw him a few months ago, and somehow, that seems strange. Maybe I thought he would be different after the journey I've been through.

"Welcome, Princess Helena," Wilhelm's father says once we're close enough. "We are honoured to have you here to formally join our family."

Melanie curtsies, and I follow suit, knowing I need to take my cues from my supposed mistress.

"Your Majesty," she responds in a voice barely above a whisper. It's probably an attempt to stop her voice from being recognised as someone who isn't me. "I'm honoured to be here."

"Why don't you come inside and rest."

"Thank you, it has been a long journey for my maid and I," she says.

I bunch my hand into a fist to fight the urge to say something. This is all wrong. I'd never greet the king and ignore Wilhelm. Not only is it wrong to do so, but I wouldn't want to.

"I didn't realise you were bringing a maid with you, I'll have someone prepare rooms," the king says.

Wilhelm's gaze lingers on me as if he can tell there's something off about the situation, a slight frown starting to mar his brow.

"It's fine, she doesn't need a room, she can sleep in the stables," Melanie says with a dismissive wave of her hand.

I wince, and not just because she wants me to sleep in the stables. It's worse that she's portraying me as some kind of callous princess who doesn't care how her servants are treated. I don't think I'm like that, but if I ever get my position back, I'm going to do everything in my power to make sure I never do again. It's not a good look on anyone.

Wilhelm's frown deepens. "Are you sure?" I can tell from the tone in his voice that he isn't impressed by that.

"Of course. Look at her. The stables are where she belongs. She should really be herding geese."

From under my lashes, I can see Wilhelm raise an eyebrow.

"Do you agree with your mistress?" he asks me softly.

I sense Melanie tense. I don't think she expected him to try talking to me, which makes sense when none of this is even about Wilhelm. She doesn't know anything about him or she'd have known he wouldn't just let her send me to the stables without saying anything.

I nod my head, though I'm screaming inside for him to realise that something's wrong.

Melanie lets out a small sigh, probably inaudible to anyone standing further away than I am.

"If you insist, then we can do that," Wilhelm says. "But there are plenty of rooms, we can draw up some for her."

"There's no need. But I would like a bath if that wouldn't be too much trouble. And an attendant to see to it."

"Do you not want your own servant?" Wilhelm asks, still not taking his eyes off me.

If I was braver, I'd look up so he can see my face properly. I'm certain he'd recognise me. But I don't want to anger Melanie for fear of what she'll do. Now we're here, she may not see the need to keep me around.

I push the thought to the side, not daring to dwell on it, nor on what it might mean for me and my continued existence.

"Of course, why don't you come inside," the King says. "One of our men will escort your servant to the stables." He gestures to a guard who makes his way over to me.

Wilhelm follows his father, but not without pausing and looking back at me.

Tears prick the corners of my eyes and threaten to fall but I blink them away. I won't let anyone see how vulnerable I feel right now.

I watch him walk away, hoping beyond anything that he can figure out what's going on and that I'm not going to be left to Melanie's mercy.

"Please follow me, miss," the guard says. "We'll try and find you a better spot tomorrow." There's pity in his voice, which definitely isn't something I expected to hear from one of Wilhelm's guards. I thought I was going to be their princess when I arrived here. Instead, I seem to be their stable girl.

If I ever manage to reverse my misfortune, I'll remember that this man spoke kindly to me. And that many of the others are bound to. It's reassuring that not all servants are as vicious and deceitful as Melanie has turned out to be.

CHAPTER 9

I study the pile of hay that's now supposed to be my bed and bite my bottom lip to keep from crying. I don't understand what I've done to Melanie. I always thought I treated her well when she was my maid, and I know my parents make sure the castle servants get a good education so they can leave service if they wish to.

Either she's punishing me for a slight I don't remember, which isn't completely impossible if

I'd been having a bad day, or she's just using me as a means to an end.

A shuffling sound from deeper in the stables makes me jump. It's going to be a long night if this is what I have to put up with the entire time. I don't think I've ever slept in a space that I shared with animals before.

Not that I suspect I'm going to get much sleep at all.

"Helena?" a familiar voice asks.

I spin around to find Wilhelm standing in the entrance of the stall I'm now supposed to be calling home.

"It is you," he says, sounding almost relieved.

"What? How? I'm sorry, will you give me a moment?" I stumble over my words, trying to work out what I can say and what I can't. I'm not sure how stringent the potion Melanie gave me is, or if it will ever wear off, but I have to assume it covers the entirety of what she's done until I can prove otherwise.

He steps towards me which is when it sinks in that he's really here and he's already said my name.

He knows I'm me.

I rush forward and throw my arms around him. His lips press against mine and we're kissing for the first time in months. For a moment, I lose myself in the feel of his love surrounding me. This is the prince I've been dreaming of coming to marry for so long, and he already knows that Melanie is pretending to be me, even if he doesn't know why.

A wave of affection floods through me. My trust in him has been well placed, and I appreciate it more than I can ever fully tell him.

We break apart, which is when it sinks in that I'm covered in all kinds of grime. I pull away from him and wave down at my dress. "I'm covered in filth," I point out. "Your stables aren't the cleanest of places."

"Do you think I care? I'm just glad to see you're safe. I was worried about you when that woman in our guest room started talking." He gestures towards my hay bale bed for the two of us to sit down.

I smooth down my skirts, already forgetting that they aren't as fine as I'm used to. Being around Wilhelm has made all of those thoughts flit out of my mind and disappear completely. I take a seat and wait for him to sit next to me before continuing our conversation.

"You knew she wasn't me?"

"Almost as soon as she showed up," he admits. "I'm annoyed at myself that I didn't know the moment she stepped out of the carriage."

I reach out and place a reassuring hand on his sleeve. "You shouldn't feel bad about that. She said that you wouldn't realise it was her until after the wedding."

"And you believed that?"

"In moments of doubt, yes," I admit, not wanting to lie to him, even about this. "But when I was thinking rationally, no. I assumed you'd be on the lookout because of my prophecy."

"I've thought about nothing else for days," he admits. "It's put a bit of a dampener on preparing for our wedding."

"Though probably not as much as finding out the bride isn't who she's supposed to be," I quip.

He chuckles. "That's true. Can you tell me who she is?"

"I don't know," I admit. "I think she's done something to stop me talking about what happened, but I'm not precisely sure what it is or what I can't say."

"That makes it hard," he observes.

I nod. "I can only tell you who I am because you guessed. And I'm still not sure what will happen if I say my name out loud."

He bunches up his fist and a flash of anger crosses over his face. "I know the most important thing is that you're here, and you're safe other than whatever is going on, but I hate that she's doing this to you."

"Me too."

"Have you figured out a way to get out of the situation?" he asks.

I shake my head. "Not yet, but I haven't had long to try and work it out, she took my place after we left Grimm Academy."

"Ah, yes, I can see how that's a problem. Did your parents not do anything to help protect you on your journey?"

I nod. "Mother sent me a charm, but she took it while I was sleeping. I don't even know if she still has it." A note of sadness enters my voice as I realise I don't have either of Mother's gifts any longer since Melanie also took her veil.

"I'll try and find out," Wilhelm promises. "Is there anything else I can do? I can set up an audience with my father if you think that will help?"

"I don't think it will," I admit. "I can't tell him what's happened even if I can see him."

"Ah, right. But I can talk about it, right?"

"I don't know." Tears spring to the corners of my eyes. "I don't know why this is happening."

Wilhelm reaches out and puts his arm around me, pulling me close to him. "It's going to be all right," he promises. "We still have time to fix this. I'm not going to marry her, I promise you that."

I lean into him and place my head on his shoulder, accepting the familiar comfort coming from him. "I know."

"And she won't get away with it. I don't know what we're able to do within the spirit of the law, but we'll find something."

"I don't even need her punishing," I whisper. "I just want my life back. I've been thinking about coming here and becoming your wife for so long, I just want it to become a reality at last."

"It will," Wilhelm promises. "We'll be married before you know it. Even if I have to run away with you and get married by a parish priest in the middle of a field of cows, I will marry you, Helena."

I let out a small laugh. "That's oddly specific."

"And oddly perfect, don't you think?"

"It does sound it," I admit. "But I don't think either of our families would go for it."

"Ah, I fear you're right. I suppose I'll just have to make do with a huge ceremony where I pledge to love you in front of all the most important people in the kingdom."

"You make it sound like such a hardship."

"Not when I have the best prize of all at the end," he counters.

I turn to face him, my heart soaring at the adoration written all over his face.

"I'm sorry this is happening to you," he whispers. "But I promise it's not enough to stop me. We'll uncover the imposter and then we'll get married and spend the rest of our lives together. I love you, Helena, and no prophecy will ever stop that being true."

"I love you too," I whisper.

He leans in and captures my lips with his, kissing me tenderly and as if there's nothing he'd rather be doing in the world.

I sink into him, feeling like things might turn out all right after all.

CHAPTER 10

The sound of someone entering the stable puts me on alert and excitement builds inside me. I didn't think Wilhelm would be back so soon, but I'm glad I am.

"Wilhelm..." I say as I turn, only to stop speaking as I recognise the veiled figure heading towards me.

"Ah, you thought your prince would have come to find you already?" Melanie taunts. She raises the veil so I can see her face.

At least she still has no idea that Wilhelm *has* come to see me already. I'm not sure what difference it really makes, but it might be helpful if she thinks she's getting away with her ruse.

"I hoped." It's not a lie in a way. I did hope that she was Wilhelm.

"Maybe if you're a good little princess, I'll let you see him after we're married. There's nothing you'll be able to do to break us up then."

I glare at her and use all my willpower not to rise to her bait, even if I want to. I still don't fully understand why she feels the need to be so cruel.

"Now, you need to tell me everything there is to know about Wilhelm's family," she says.

I let out an unladylike snort. "Why would I help you to deceive Wilhelm's family? They've been nothing but good to me."

"And yet they haven't noticed you've been replaced, how sad."

Was she like this when she was my lady's maid? I don't remember her being so cruel, but that doesn't really mean anything. I'm sure servants keep plenty of things from their masters, including their true selves.

"I don't have time to tell you everything even if I wanted to," I point out. "We're talking about eleven years of knowing one another. Weekly letters, regular visits. How am I going to tell you all of that in a short space of time?"

"Well you've got to do *something*, or I'm going to get found out." Melanie's frustration is written all over her face.

"Has it crossed your mind that I might want you to find out?" If she is, then someone is bound to wonder where I am and they'll find me eventually. Especially if Wilhelm starts to spend more time down in the stables.

"You're going to help me or I'm going to make your dear Wilhelm's life miserable. I can start by making him think you never loved him. After that, I'll move on to making him think that you resent him for making you leave your kingdom to move to his."

I raise an eyebrow. "Is that the best you've got?" Never mind the fact Wilhelm has already figured out that she's not me, but he isn't going to believe any of that at all. He knows I love him, and he knows that I've come to terms with leaving my kingdom behind because we've talked about it. Something that Melanie doesn't seem to have deemed possible.

It's becoming clear that it isn't just about me, it seems to be about Wilhelm and his family too. Or at least royalty in general. I suppose that to some extent it doesn't matter what made it happen. She decided to take a chance on making my prophecy come true because it's the one she learned about first.

"What are you planning on doing after the wedding?" I ask. "They'll know you aren't me, then."

"Who says that's true?"

"You don't look anything like me," I point out. "And you can't keep wearing a veil, especially around Wilhelm. They're going to figure it out."

"Then I'll just have to find a way to postpone the wedding until I can find a way to make sure they don't discover that I'm not you. Or maybe it'll be easier to make Wilhelm fall in love with me, that can't be too hard."

"It's not as simple as getting Wilhelm to love you, there's a treaty between our kingdoms to take into account." I'm not meaning to give her more information, but it seems like the necessary way to keep her talking so I can assess what she's going to do and the best way to fix the problem she's created. There has to be some hole in her plan that we can take advantage of.

"But you were tragically lost on the way to marry your prince. The treaty isn't broken, it's only made stronger because of the shared grief." Her lips curl up into a satisfied smile, like she genuinely thinks that's going to be enough.

But it does reveal that she has no idea that Wilhelm knows about my prophecy, or she'd be more worried about him working things out.

I hope.

"It doesn't matter, I have time to think about this while I postpone your wedding, and you have time to realise that you need to start helping me or something very bad could happen to you."

"As opposed to the little bit bad they are already?" I counter.

"You're alive, and have use of all of your limbs. Consider how things could be worse and I'll come see if you're ready to reevaluate things in a couple of days." She turns on her heels and stalks off without waiting for me to respond, though that may be a good thing. The words I have in mind for her aren't particularly princess-like, though I suppose I'm not a princess right now.

I stare after her with a growing determination to fix the problem, and I don't want to waste any time doing it.

The urge to see Wilhelm overwhelms me, but it takes me a moment to realise that I'm just a servant now. I can slip through the castle mostly unnoticed, and I already know where Wilhelm's room is.

Without thinking twice about it, I head out of the stables and towards the main castle. Hopefully I'm able to find my way without getting too lost.

And once I do, I'll be able to talk to Wilhelm and come up with a plan to put all of this behind us.

CHAPTER 11

S neaking up to Wilhelm's room in the middle of the night feels dangerous, but also kind of exciting at the same time. A small part of me wonders if I'd have been doing this even if things had gone smoothly and I'd arrived at the castle as myself. I don't imagine Wilhelm and Melanie are getting to spend much one-on-one time together now everyone is watching them as an about-to-be-wedded couple.

I knock on the door and wait nervously for him to answer. I'm not sure why I thought this was a good idea without checking with him first, but there aren't many chances for us to cross paths. I suspect he'll be trying everything he can to come down to the stables, while Melanie will be doing everything she can in order to keep him away. She has to realise that Wilhelm recognising me is the riskiest part of her plan.

The heavy wooden door swings open and Wilhelm's face appears. Confusion turns to delight as he realises it's me.

"You shouldn't be here," he says. "We'll get into trouble." Despite his words, he reaches out and pulls me inside.

"And what will happen if we get caught? Will they force us to get married?" I ask with a raised eyebrow.

Confusion flits over his face, followed by under-standing. "Well that's one way to solve the prob-lem. I can't marry your imposter if I already have to marry you."

"It'd cause a mild scandal until someone realised who I am," I point out.

"Hmm. Good point, though I think Father is suspicious. He was talking to your impersonator about some of the trips to your kingdom, and she gave him strange answers."

"Isn't that what you said tipped you off?"

"It is."

"Huh." I sit down on the edge of his bed, trying not to think about where I am. This isn't how I thought I'd first be seeing his bedroom. "Is there a chance she hasn't done enough research on me before taking my place?"

Wilhelm nods and comes to join me on the bed, being careful to keep enough distance between us that it's proper.

"I'd have thought she'd be better at lying when answering those questions though," I admit. "She was my maid during many of the visits."

"I don't know what to tell you," Wilhelm responds. "But she's making herself look bad."

"And by that you mean she's making *me* look bad," I mutter.

He winces. "I'm sorry, I know that can't be easy."

"It's fine. I know it'll be all right once she's revealed as an imposter." Maybe. For all I know, the switch back will happen privately and no one will know that I was replaced, even for a short amount of time.

"Not that I'm not glad you're here, but did you come for a reason?" he asks.

I nod. "I had the first inkling of a plan when my imposter was trying to force more information out of me earlier."

"She did that?" Anger lingers in Wilhelm's voice.

I reach out and place a gentle hand on his leg, trying not to focus on how dirty I look right now. "She didn't hurt me physically, and I didn't give her any useful information." I don't think.

"All right, then I'll let that one slide for now. What was your plan?"

"It was about trying to make it so your father figures out that she's not the real Helena. If you think he's already suspicious, then that's a good thing, it'll make it easier."

Wilhelm nods. "I don't think it'll take much to convince him. But it's hard when she refuses to let anyone see her face."

"Because there's still that small element of doubt that she's lying," I say.

"Precisely."

"What if we didn't do that?"

"Persuade Father she's an imposter? Isn't that the entire point?"

"It is. But what if we did the opposite and tried to persuade him that I'm the real Helena."

"Ahh." Understanding dawns on his face. "I can see that working."

"Especially if he's already confused by some of her answers."

"But how are we going to do that?"

"Do you remember which visits your father asked her about?"

"Of course," Wilhelm responds. "Why?"

"What if you brought him down to the stables tomorrow and talked about one of them and I can interject with something only real Helena would know?" It's a risk, especially if his father doesn't want to be talked to by a servant girl.

"It might work, but I don't see why I can't just tell him that you're the real Helena, especially if he already thinks you have an imposter. He does know about your prophecy."

I bite my bottom lip. There's something tempting about that course of events, but it also worries me that there's more potential for things to go wrong. "But you barely know anything."

"Because you won't tell me."

"Because I can't," I correct. "I drank a potion that stops me from talking about what my imposter did, or who I am."

"And who she is?"

I shrug. "That's the worst part, I don't know. She didn't tell me the exact way it worked and I just have to guess which parts I can talk about safely and which I can't."

"Hmm. That complicates things."

"It makes it feel impossible," I admit in a whisper.

He shuffles closer to me and pulls me into his arms. For a moment, I accept the comfort he wants to offer, forgetting completely about the dirt on my clothes and the soreness invading my body from not being able to sleep on a proper bed. If Melanie wants to punish me for an unknown crime, then she's doing an excellent job at it. I feel wretched even without knowing that she's tricking people I care about.

"I know it feels as if it can't be fixed, but it can," Wilhelm promises. "I'll bring Father down to the stables tomorrow while your imposter has tea with my mother. But if he doesn't come to the right conclusion, then I'm going to tell him that I think you're Helena and that there's an imposter in the palace."

"But we don't know what will happen to me if I talk about who I am," I whisper.

"Then I will send for every wise woman or healer in the city to try and work out what you've been given and how to reverse it. And if none of them know, then I'll search the entire kingdom until we have an antidote to give you. One day, we'll look back at this as nothing more than a vague memory of the time we stopped your prophecy from coming true."

I sniff as tears start to fall. I hurriedly wipe them away, not wanting to let him see how much this is getting to me.

I'm scared, more so than I'm willing to admit to myself. I know all of my friends have gone through their prophecies and come out the other side un-harmed, but they all had other people around them, and they were at Grimm, a place they knew. I'm alone save for Wilhelm, and no one is any the wiser about what's going on. I want my friends to be here even more than I thought I would.

"You can cry if you want to," Wilhelm says. "I can't imagine how hard this is." He tightens his hold on me, which is just as well as his words force the dam to open and heaving sobs rip through me.

He doesn't pull away or act repulsed. If anything he holds me tighter and rocks me as he hums an unfamiliar tune.

But I don't think I'm just crying because I'm scared, or because it's a horrible situation. I think I'm also crying because I can see that I'm not completely out of hope. And that, despite it seeming like my prophecy may have won, there's still hope for me to end up exactly where I want to be. In Wilhelm's arms and being able to call him my husband.

I just need to have a little more patience.

CHAPTER 12

Every time I hear someone enter the stables, nerves flutter in my stomach as I prepare for the potentially difficult conversation to come. I don't dislike Wilhelm's father, but the relationship between a princess and a king is very different from that of a servant and her sovereign. If he doesn't want to listen to me, then we may end up right back at the beginning with no chance of a reprieve. Ending up as a goose girl in Wilhelm's

country for the rest of my life is going to be tor-
ture. I'll always have to see him from afar, and I'll
certainly never get to travel to see my family or my
friends.

And all I'll have with Wilhelm is stolen moments
while Melanie will be his wife in every way.

I take a steadying breath and continue to sweep
the stable floor. No one has given me a proper job
to do, so I'm just trying to make myself generally
useful. I don't know if it's because they can sense
that there's something off about me, or if they
think that Melanie may change her mind about
wanting her own servant from her own kingdom
again.

Honestly, I don't think it particularly matters.
For now, I don't have anything specific to do,
which is making things both easier and harder. I
think I'd rather be so busy that I don't have time
to think about all of the ways this can go wrong.

The stable door creaks and I look up to find Wilhelm and his father entering. Wilhelm shoots me a quick smile, sending my heart into a flutter as he does. They move through the stables, admiring all of the horses and making their way towards where I am. I know Wilhelm will be doing it this way in order to make it seem natural and not forced.

Despite understanding *why* he's doing it, the waiting isn't any easier.

"Do you remember that time when we visited Helena's kingdom and you got lost in the orchard?" Wilhelm asks his father once they're within hearing distance.

The king chuckles. "I do. You must have been all of ten years old."

A smile comes to my face as I recall the memory.

"There was a woman singing. I don't remember how the song goes," Wilhelm says, glancing over at me.

I take that as my cue and start humming the song I know he's referring to.

A wistful expression flits over his father's face. "How did it go again? *There was a little milkmaid, her arms laden with pails.*"

"*She trekked over the hills and dales,*" I sing softly.

The king turns and stares at me.

Nerves make it feel as if I'm about to explode, but I keep singing the song, never too loud. At least my voice is passable, though it has nothing on some of the people I've known.

"How do you know that song?" he asks.

"They sing it in my hometown, Your Majesty."

"It isn't a song anyone sings here," he responds.

"No, Your Majesty. I'm not from here."

He narrows his eyes.

"Didn't you arrive recently from Grimm Academy?" Wilhelm asks.

"I did, Your Highness."

"Did you attend classes?" the king asks.

"Yes."

"And yet you're in the stables." Something in his tone suggests that he's starting to put things into place. I don't think he's going to be able to get straight to the fact I'm the one who is supposed to be marrying his son, but the suspicion that I'm somewhere I shouldn't be is a good start.

Unless it gets me executed. But I'll cross that bridge if I come to it.

"I'm not here by choice, Your Majesty," I admit. "But this seems to be where the fates have had me end up."

Is that too close to mentioning a prophecy? I'm not sure. But Wilhelm is nodding as if I've said the right thing.

"This is the maid that was ordered to sleep in the stables," Wilhelm says.

His father frowns. "Does that seem like an odd request on the part of the princess to you?"

I hold my breath, not daring to say anything.

"It seemed very out of character," Wilhelm says. "She hasn't been acting like herself since she got here."

"Hmm. True. I put it down to pre-wedding nerves, but that doesn't seem like the Helena I've met before. She was always very taken by you."

"And I by her," Wilhelm agrees. "I wouldn't want to marry anyone but the true Helena."

My eyes widen. If he isn't careful, he's going to end up giving something away that he shouldn't.

I shake my head ever so slightly to remind him to be careful, but I have no idea if it's enough to persuade him into silence.

"There's definitely something going on," the king says. "Perhaps I should have a little chat with the princess today."

"I think that's an excellent idea," Wilhelm responds. "In fact, you should go summon her now. I'll take care of telling the grooms what you need for Fennel."

The king nods. "Excellent idea. Make sure they give Fennel those carrots he likes."

I soften towards my future father-in-law. He's normally a lot more proper than this, but it seems that he has a soft spot for his horse, and for his son.

Neither Wilhelm or I say anything as we wait for him to disappear.

"Do you think that's going to be enough?" I ask him once we're sure we're alone.

"Honestly, I'm not sure. I expected him to ask you more about your kingdom after the song."

"Maybe that's all he needed?" Even as I say it, I get jittery. I can't believe we're pinning all of our hopes on a song the king heard eight years ago.

"I think so," Wilhelm assures me. "He's not going to let your imposter off easily with the questions now. I wouldn't be surprised if he knows the truth in a matter of hours."

I take a shaky breath. "Do you really think so?"

He nods. "And then we'll be able to get married."

"I can't wait," I say in response.

"Me neither." He reaches out and pulls me to him.

"Wilhelm, what if someone sees?" I whisper, though I secretly love it.

"Then they'll think I'm taking advantage of the new stable girl."

"That's not a good thing," I point out.

"It isn't," he agrees. "But it'll make them turn a blind eye for a moment and I'm all right with that if you are?"

I chuckle and go up on my tiptoes to press a swift kiss against his lips. "That's all you're getting for now," I assure him.

"It'll do until you're properly back on my arm."

My heart flutters in my chest. I hope he's right about his father because I don't think I'll be able to take much more of clandestine kisses and stolen moments.

CHAPTER 13

My skin is pink and raw from the heat of the baths, but I don't care. I'm glad to be clean for the first time in a few days. I'm not sure why Wilhelm sent a message for me to be summoned for a bath, but I'm grateful for him doing it. And for the clean dress waiting for me. It isn't as fine as my own wardrobe is, but it's certainly better than the ill-fitting servant's dress Melanie gave me.

"Follow me," a housemaid says as soon as I'm done.

I frown but do as she says, knowing it's better for me if I listen to the house servants. They're the ones who have the ability to make my life a misery. Though so far, the few I've spoken to have all been polite, much to my relief.

She stops in front of a door I don't recognise. I don't think this is part of the castle I've been in during my other visits. "You're expected," she says.

A guard opens the door and ushers me inside.

Confusion wars within me as I step into a cosy but ornate room. It only takes me a moment to put the pieces together and realise I'm in the more intimate dining area of the royal family. While they aren't alone, they have only their most trusted advisers and guests with them. This is where I'd likely have been eating had I not been tricked by Melanie.

"Helena," the king says warmly, getting up from his seat and opening his arms to me.

I pause in my place, unsure what to do. as he envelops me in a hug.

I catch Wilhelm's eyes, and he just smiles smugly, as if a plan has come together.

"Please accept our apologies for not recognising you when you first arrived," the king says. "And take your seat by Wilhelm, where you should have been the entire time."

Ah, I see. He's realised who I am and is now presumably trying to influence me so I don't tell my parents I've been mistreated. Not that it will make much difference. I haven't been mistreated by anyone except Melanie, and she's from my own kingdom.

"Before you do, there's someone I'd like you to meet," Wilhelm says, gesturing to the side.

One of the guards enters followed by an elderly woman with the look of wisdom about her.

"This is a local Hedge Witch who believes she can sort out the problem of you not being able to say anything about what happened," Wilhelm says.

Affection floods through me as I realise how hard he must have had to work to find her.

"Why don't we take a seat over here, dear?" the woman says, gesturing for a seat by the window.

I glance at the king who just nods, seeming a little surprised but not opposed to me going with her.

I take a seat and fold my hands demurely on my lap as the woman mutters a small incantation and a filmy bubble of magic surrounds us.

Nerves flutter within me as I wonder what it's for.

"What's your name, dear?" the old woman asks.

"I-I can't say."

She smiles kindly at me. "That's where you're wrong. You can say your name within the bubble." She gestures to the shiny shield around us. "It temporarily suspends curses and other malevolent magic."

"That's possible?"

"It's an old Hedge Witch secret." She grins almost as if she knows she's letting me in on a big secret. "If you tell me your name and your story, I can concoct a potion that will reverse the damage done."

I stare at her for a moment. "Are you certain?"

She nods. "But beware, it will only work if you tell the complete truth. You won't be able to lie about any part of the story after you drink this."

"I don't want to anyway."

"I didn't think so. The king said you were honest."

"Oh." I never realised he thought so highly of me beyond my political pedigree.

"Now, your name," she prompts.

"Helena."

"It's nice to meet you, Helena." She spins something through the air around us. "Why don't you tell me everything that happened?"

I nod and launch into a recount of everything that happened since I received Wilhelm's letter. It's a relief to be able to say it all out loud, especially after worrying about not being able to, and there's still a part of me that worries she isn't telling me the truth about her magic and I'll face the consequences of speaking out about Melanie.

But I have to maintain my faith. Magic can be used for good as well as bad, and I shouldn't let my experience with a prophecy determine how I feel about the entire practice.

A small ball of light forms in front of the wise woman as I talk.

"I think that's it," she says once I'm done. She directs the light ball into two small bottles already standing waiting. She picks one up and shakes it a few times. "Drink this and then you'll be able to tell nothing about the truth about the situation. There won't be any consequences from the curse your imposter placed on you."

I eye the bottle warily. "Are you sure?"

"With magic anything is possible, but I'm as sure as I can be."

I nod and drink down the potion, certain that there's no other option for me anyway.

"What's the other one for?" I ask.

"Your imposter. If you give it to her, she won't be able to lie either." She hands it to me. "But you don't have to use it if you don't want to."

"Thank you for your help."

She smiles and waves away the bubble. "Go forth as a free woman, Helena."

I rise to my feet and make my way over to the top table where the king and Wilhelm wait.

"It worked," I say. "I'm the real Helena." The moment it slips from my lips I feel like crying in relief.

Wilhelm jumps to his feet and pulls me into his arms, spinning me around. He's one step away from kissing me, though I know that would be frowned upon by some of the more conservative people in the room.

"Is it over?"

"Not quite," I point out. "Unless you did something to Melanie without me knowing about it?"

"Melanie? I recognise her name."

"You should, she was my maid when you visited a few times," I remind him.

"Ah, right." He leads me back to our seats at the table. "But no, we thought you might like to see her face the moment that she realises she's failed."

"What will happen to her?"

"That depends. I think at the very least imprisonment, but it depends what she ends up charged with and by who. I think there's a prison who will take prisoners who have tried to make prophecies come true, but that's only if Father doesn't decide to punish her here for the laws she broke in our kingdom."

"Do you think he'll do that?"

"Potentially. He isn't happy with the disrespect shown to either you or us in her plot."

Which is understandable and not something I think she thought through. I imagine Melanie thought she'd be untouchable once she married Wilhelm.

As if summoned by our thoughts, a set of double doors opened and Melanie stepped in wearing one of my best ball gowns. It's completely wrong for the kind of dinner we're currently at, which I'd have thought she'd known through her training as a maid, but apparently not.

Wilhelm reaches out under the table and takes my hand in his, giving it a squeeze to let me know that everything is going to be all right.

Melanie heads in our direction, causing the tension to build within me. I have no idea how she's going to react to me being sat in her place. Well, my place that she stole in the first place. But that isn't going to be the way she sees it. Not when she's already doing this because she's angry at me for something that doesn't really make sense.

"What is my maid doing here?" she demands loud enough for everyone in the room to hear.

"I think you know the answer to that," the king responds, a thread of a threat through his words. I don't think I'd want to be on the receiving end of that tone of voice.

"I don't know what you could possibly mean," she responds. "She should be in the stables where I sent her." There's a hint of uncertainty in her voice, as if she doesn't know for sure whether to continue the charade.

"I'd like to request that you remove your veil, please," the king says.

"What? No. It's tradition in my kingdom that my betrothed never sees my face."

One glance at the king reveals just how little patience he has left for the woman pretending to be me.

"You will remove your veil so we can see that you are Princess Helena, though I suspect we shall discover that you are not."

Even with the heavy veil still covering her face I can sense her gaze directed at me.

"If you don't remove the veil yourself, then one of my guards will do it for you," the king says. "So I suggest that you comply sooner rather than later."

Shaking hands lift the fabric so it's over her face.

Several people around the table gasp, though I'm not sure why when they're already aware that I'm seated among them.

"Guards, arrest her and return the veil to the true Princess Helena." He gestures for them.

Melanie turns on her heels and starts to head towards the open doors, but she's already been caught up to by guards. Two of them restrain her while another removes the veil with surprisingly careful fingers. He carefully brings it over to me and places it down.

"Thank you," I croak. "I have this." I hold out the second bottle the Hedge Witch gave me.

"What is it?" the guard asks.

"Magic that will make it so she can't lie about her impersonation of me. You can use it if you wish to."

"Thank you, Your Highness."

"My gratitude is to you for removing the imposter from my place," I respond. "And for treating me kindly when I was nothing more than a lonely maid."

He does a double-take, probably not having connected me to the woman he showed to the stables when I first arrived. "I'm sorry, Your Highness, I didn't recognise you then..."

"It's no problem," I assure him. "Your kindness was much appreciated after a trying time."

He dips his head in response and takes the bottle from me, returning to his fellow guards.

Melanie kicks and screams as she's dragged away. Once the doors close behind her and we're left in blissful silence the king gets to his feet and raises his goblet of wine.

"To the true Princess Helena, my future daughter-in-law," he calls out.

"To Princess Helena," the room echoes as a furious blush spreads over my cheeks at the attention.

"To my future wife," Wilhelm adds softly, reminding me that I have someone by my side who will support me as I try to regain a sense of normalcy in my life.

While I wish Melanie hadn't stolen my life, I'm lucky in that the people around me noticed and helped me to do something about it. My friends may be back at Grimm Academy, but I'm far from alone in my new kingdom, and this has proven it beyond anything I could possibly imagine.

EPILOGUE

A knock on the door pulls me from my wedding preparations. I react instantly, before remembering that I'm supposed to trust the staff to do things like this now.

"Could you get it, please?" I ask my new maid.

"Of course, Your Highness."

I watch her carefully as she makes her way across the room, already worrying about what's going to happen and if she might turn on me. I know it isn't likely, especially after the stringent checks put into place following everything that happened.

She pulls the door open and steps aside as four familiar faces rush into the room, each of them dressed exquisitely as befits coming to a wedding.

It takes me a moment to realise my friends are really here. I jump to my feet and rush over to them, barely thinking about my clothing as they hug me to them.

"We heard about everything," Briar says.

"The whole academy is abuzz with everything. Did you hear that there were two attempts to make your prophecy come true?" Ella says.

I nod. "The headmistress wrote to me. She says I have Princess Alyeesah to thank for saving me from the first attempt."

"Well, just Aly," Rapunzel says. "It turns out that she's not actually a princess, but she gets to stay at Grimm Academy because she helped you avoid your prophecy."

"If only it had been as simple as that," I mutter.

"Have you heard anything about Melanie since?" Ella asks.

"Not really. She's in the prison reserved for people who try to make prophecies come true, but that's all I know. Wilhelm thought that his father might want to punish her here, but he thought it was better if he handed her over," I say.

"It must be a relief."

I nod. "It is. I'm glad it's over. I understand how you all feel about your prophecies now."

Briar chuckles. "I'm not surprised."

"What are you doing here, anyway? I thought you'd be in class. Not that I want you to leave. Please stay," I ramble.

"Wilhelm invited us," Marigold says brightly. "He saw that you were upset about the prophecy,

Melanie, and leaving us behind, so he sent a letter asking for us to come to your wedding."

"That's so sweet," I whisper, clutching my hands to my chest. "I can't believe I get to marry him."

"You'd better start because you're doing it in five minutes," Ella says.

"Oh yes, will you get my veil?" I ask.

"Are you still wearing it?" Rapunzel seems surprised, and I don't blame her.

"A small part of me wants to forgo it, but it's an important tradition from my kingdom and Mother sent it to me. I want to wear it for her. But I had the castle seamstresses make a few changes, I think you'll approve of them."

Ella hands me the heavy lace and I turn to the mirror, setting it on the small tiara that's been designed just for this.

"It's beautiful," Marigold says.

"Thank you." The veil frames my face, but doesn't cover it. I thought it would be better for all of us if everyone can see that it's me underneath it.

Another knock sounds on the door and my maid goes to open it without instruction. "We're ready for the princess," a man says.

"I'm ready," I tell her.

"We'll see you at the reception," Briar says, reaching out to give my hand a squeeze.

"I'm so glad you came."

"We are too." Ella's genuine smile gives an undeniable sense of truth to the words.

They hurry out of the room, leaving me lighter than ever. Not only do I get to marry the prince I love today, and I get to do it with my best friends around me. Nothing could be better.

I leave the room and make my way to the back of the chapel. Hundreds of people line either side of the room, but I don't have eyes for them. The only person I can focus on is Wilhelm waiting for me at the bottom of the aisle with a wide smile on his face.

Music starts to play and I begin the walk to the altar, wishing I could go faster but knowing this is one of those occasions where the way I act matters.

"You look beautiful," Wilhelm whispers the moment I reach him and he takes my hands in his. "Especially in the veil."

"I'm glad you like it. I wanted to make it my own."

"You did a good job," he agrees. "But I'm really glad I can see it's really you I'm going to marry."

I let out a small laugh, receiving a scolding look from the priest in response.

Wilhelm suppresses a smile and the two of us face the front, ready to get married. Excitement bubbles within me as we exchange our vows and keep casting one another hidden looks when we think no one's watching.

Not that I'm paying much attention to anyone else. I know my friends are here and in the crowd, but they don't matter right now.

"You may seal this union with a kiss," the priest announces.

Wilhelm turns to me and leans in, brushing his lips against mine. The fleeting kiss is enough to set me all aflutter.

"That was our first kiss," Wilhelm whispers teasingly once he's pulled back. "As far as everyone else knows."

I smother a laugh. "Then they're fools for believing it."

No one can hear us over the sounds of the cheering, but I don't think that matters. The only thing I can focus on is the feel of my hand in Wilhelm's and the knowledge that everything is going to be fine from now on.

I may have had a prophecy, but we managed to safely avoid it and get to where we want to be.

Now it's time to start my happy ever after with Wilhelm by my side.

***

Thank you for reading *Feathers Of Fate*, I hope you enjoyed it. If you want to continue the series, you can in *The Almost Queen*, a retelling of the Guinevere and Lancelot legend.

Author Note

Thank you for reading *Feathers of Fate*, I hope you enjoyed it!

It's hard for me to believe that the *Once Upon An Academy* series is over, but as Helena's story has been in the works since the very first *Grimm Academy* book, it feels like the right place to stop it. She's been waiting for her story for a while now! If you're new to the Grimm World with this book, then you may want to check out Helena's friends' stories in *Spindles and Spells* (Briar), *Pumpkins and Proms* (Ella), *Tower Of Thorns* (Rapunzel), and *Lilies Of Loss* (Marigold), where each of them takes on their prophecy. You can also read about the events on the bridge from another perspective in *Lamps and Lies* (a gender-flipped Aladdin retelling).

If you've read *Lamps and Lies* then you may wonder why I didn't make Fatin the antagonist in *Feathers Of Fate*, especially as that would still have fit with the fairy tale I chose. The honest answer is that I actually did plan it that way, but when it came time to write Helena's story, I realised that it would work a lot better a different way, especially as having Fatin as the antagonist wouldn't have given Helena much to do, and would have given Wilhelm very little page time, which I felt was unfair for him when he's been a mentioned character for so long!

The Grimm World will continue with *Princess Of Petals*, part of the new *Princess Competition* mini-series.

While I know the Goose Girl isn't a hugely well-known fairy tale, it's one I wanted to do because it's a favourite of one of my friends. While it's not a fairy tale I've ever been overly familiar with, I thought that it also provided a rich amount of interesting inspiration - and that's something I can never turn down when it comes to doing a fairy tale retelling.

If you want to keep up to date with new releases and other news, you can join my <u>Facebook Reader Group</u> or <u>mailing list</u>.

Stay safe & happy reading!

- Laura

Also By Laura Greenwood

Signed Paperback & Merchandise:

You can find signed paperbacks, hardcovers, and merchandise based on my series (including stickers, magnets, face masks, and more!) via my website.

Series List:

* denotes a completed series

The Obscure World

A paranormal & urban fantasy world where supernaturals live out in the open alongside humans. Each series can be read on its own, but there are cameos from past characters and mentions of previous events.

<u>Cauldron Coffee Shop</u> - <u>Broomstick Bakery</u> - <u>Obscure Academy</u> - <u>The Shifter Season</u> - <u>Grimalkin Academy</u>* - <u>City Of Blood</u>* - <u>Grimalkin Vampires</u>* - <u>Supernatural Retrieval Agency</u>* - <u>The Black Fan</u>* - <u>Sabre Woods Academy</u>* - <u>Scythe Grove Academy</u>* – <u>Ashryn Barker</u>*

The Forgotten Gods World

A fantasy romance world based on Egyptian mythology.

<u>Forgotten God</u>

The Egyptian Empire

A modern fantasy world set in an alternative timeline where the Egyptian Empire never fell.

The Apprentice Of Anubis

The Paranormal Council Universe

A paranormal romance & urban fantasy world where paranormals are hidden away from the human world, and are in search of their fated mates. Each series can be read on its own, but there are cameos from past characters and mentions of previous events.

The Paranormal Council Series* - The Fae of the Paranormal Council Universe* - Paranormal Criminal Investigations* - The Necromancer Council*

Other Series

Purple Oasis (with Arizona Tape) - Grimm Academy - Beyond The Curse* - Untold Tales* - The Dragon Duels* - Speed Dating With The Denizens Of The Underworld (shared world) - Seven Wardens* (with Skye MacKinnon) - Tales Of Clan Robbins (co-written with L.A. Boruff) - Firehouse Witches* (with Lacey Carter Andersen & L.A. Boruff) - Mountain Shifters* (with Lainie Anderson)

Twin Souls Universe

A paranormal romance & urban fantasy world co-written with Arizona Tape. Each series can be read on its own, but there are cameos from past characters and mentions of previous events.

Amethyst's Wand Shop Mysteries - Twin Souls* - The Vampire Detective*

About Laura Greenwood

Laura is a USA Today Bestselling Author of paranormal, fantasy, urban fantasy, and contemporary romance. When she's not writing, she drinks a lot of tea, tries to resist French macarons, and works towards a diploma in Egyptology. She lives in the UK, where most of her books are set. Laura specialises in quick reads, whether you're looking for a swoonworthy romance for the bath, or an action-packed adventure for your latest journey, you'll find the perfect match amongst her books!

Follow Laura Greenwood

Website: www.authorlauragreenwood.co.uk

Mailing List: https://www.authorlauragreenwood.co.uk/p/book-sign-up.html

Facebook Group: http://facebook.com/groups/theparanormalcouncil

Facebook Page: http://facebook.com/authorlauragreenwood

Bookbub: www.bookbub.com/authors/laura-greenwood